"Everyone knows about Jacob," his father said.

Paul felt a shudder run through his entire body. He imagined all of Brasston knowing about Jacob; he thought of what George would say, George who said the worst, most comical things about the teachers, the kids in class, strangers on the sidewalks—things that made Paul double over with laughter.

His father picked up one of Paul's sneakers from the floor and began to turn it slowly in his hand.

"It will be different—if we're *seen* together," Paul said after a moment.

"Do you think other people have no troubles?" his father asked suddenly.

Paul didn't answer.

"We need your help. You can't go on forever as if you don't have a brother," his father said. He let the sneaker drop onto the floor.

PAULA FOX won the Newbery Medal for *The Slave Dancer*, the American Book Award for *A Place Apart*, and the Hans Christian Andersen Medal and the Empire State Award for her collected work for children. Among her other novels are *The Eagle Kite; Monkey Island; Western Wind*, a *Boston Globe–Horn Book* Honor Book; *The Village by the Sea*, winner of a *Boston Globe–Horn Book* Award; and *One-Eyed Cat*, a Newbery Honor Book.

Paula Fox lives in Brooklyn, New York.

ALSO BY PAULA FOX

Radiance Descending

a novel by

PAULA FOX

Published by
Bantam Doubleday Dell Books for Young Readers
a division of
Random House, Inc.
1540 Broadway
New York, New York 10036

The trademark Laurel-Leaf Library® is registered in the U.S. Patent and Trademark Office.
The trademark Dell® is registered in the U.S. Patent and Trademark Office.

Visit us on the Web! www.randomhouse.com/teens

Educators and librarians, for a variety of teaching tools, visit us at www.randomhouse.com/teachers

ISBN: 0-440-22748-8

RL: 6.3

Reprinted by arrangement with DK Publishing, Inc.

Printed in the United States of America

December 1999

10 9 8 7 6 5 4 3 2

OPM

For Jaimee,

Dan,

Nicole,

and Tobias

CONTENTS

HIM

Him. Doing what he did every school morning. Waving from the living room window. Jacob the booby, his eyeglasses aslant on his little fat nose, a sweater or a T-shirt—whatever he'd pulled over his head—on backward, toast crumbs from breakfast sticking to his upper lip.

Paul, his elder brother, his hands gripping the straps of his backpack as he walked down the path from the house, didn't wave back.

He didn't have to see Jacob to know that he was

at the window, or to see their mother, Nora Coleman, to know she was standing a few feet behind him. She watched everything Jacob did. When he ate, her mouth opened and closed as though she ate with him. When he cried, her face crumpled. When he laughed, mostly about nothing as far as Paul could see, she laughed, too. Of course she would have seen Jacob run to the window and would have followed him.

Later, in the afternoon when Paul came home from school and raced into the kitchen through the back door, forgetting that Jacob had ever been born, she was there to remind him.

"Please," she said. "Turn around and look at Jacob when you go to school in the mornings. It will make him happy. You don't even have to smile."

Paul was silent, as he usually was when his mother or father asked him directly to do something for Jacob.

"It's mean," she said. "You're stuck in meanness, Paul."

He would not wave the next morning, or the morning after that. The moment his parents asked him to do more for Jacob than live with him under the same roof, he felt he was drowning in a stagnant, slimy pond in a dark forest where there was no one to save him.

When Jacob got into Paul's things, or threw a pillow in his direction, or stuck a spoon into his dessert, Paul's throat unlocked and he had plenty to say. He could protest loudly and feel righteous. But when Jacob behaved in a way their mother and father called "sweet," and Paul was supposed to do something about it, he felt himself sinking into the black water of that pond, his mouth stopped up with wet weeds.

One Friday morning in early April, Paul strode down the cement path to the street, where the school bus would stop to pick him up. Overnight a forsythia bush had bloomed, and one long, arched branch brushed his face irritatingly. It could have been Jacob touching him with a grubby finger. He walked faster, keeping his gaze on his feet as, hard step by hard step, they took him farther away from his parents, from Jacob and the slow back-and-forth movement of his left hand, from a smile that made his eyes squeeze shut. A year-round pumpkin on the windowsill.

At the end of the month, on April 30, Jacob would turn seven. He would look the same when he was

Paul's age, eleven, only taller and bulkier. By that time Paul intended to be as far away from home as he could get.

He heard the front door slam, the pounding of feet on the path. Suddenly he was seized by his shoulders and held rigid.

"Paul!" his father exclaimed.

Keeping a grip on Paul's shoulders, he turned him around as though he were setting a screw into wood until Paul was facing the house and the window against which Jacob was pressing his broad, freckled forehead.

"Wave back!" his father commanded him. "I swear this has got to stop! Do it!"

"I can't," Paul cried out.

"You mean you won't," his father said angrily.

He took hold of Paul's arm and moved it up and down like a lever. "Look at your brother! You'll do this from now on—do you understand?"

Jacob was laughing in his wild way, jumping up and down, waving both his hands with excitement.

Paul heard a rumble of wheels, a whoosh of brakes. His father released him abruptly, and Paul fled to the yellow bus, its door opening. He leaped up the steps into the close, breathy air. His friends shouted greetings, the driver shifted gears, the door closed. Paul felt as if a great stone had rolled off his back.

For the better part of the day he would not think about Jacob. He would not think about his mother and father who, where Jacob was concerned, had become his enemies.

JACOB COMES HOME

On a morning nearly seven years earlier, Jacob, wrapped up to his nose in a blue blanket, was carried into the living room of the New York City apartment where Paul and his parents, Dr. and Mrs. Coleman, then lived. Paul had just won a game of checkers he had played with Grandpa Coleman. Grandpa didn't pretend to lose as Paul knew Daddy did. When Paul finished off Grandpa's kings, it was a true victory.

"Here's Jacob," Grandpa said, looking at Paul.

His mother was looking at him, too. "Here's your brother," she said softly. "And here am I."

He felt shy; he hadn't seen Mom for a week. He looked down at the checkerboard, smiling. When he looked up, he saw that the baby's blanket had fallen away from his head. He appeared to be blowing an enormous, white bubble that hid most of his face. "Oh!" Mom exclaimed. She went with Daddy into their bedroom. He could see her through the doorway. She had put Jacob down in Paul's old crib and was wiping his mouth with a cloth while he squealed like a puppy.

At the sound, Paul felt a small shock, as though he'd touched a sliver of glass. He started to set up the checker pieces again.

Grandpa said, "I have something to tell you."

He spoke in a plain, level voice that had the effect of a steadying hand. Paul had no idea of what was coming, but he gazed across the board at him. When Grandpa saw he had Paul's attention, he folded his big knobby hands in his lap.

"Your new brother has a condition," he began. "It has a name. Down syndrome. Medical words are not beautiful. What you need to know is that he won't learn things the way you do. He'll be slow. You'll have to learn patience. When I was a college student, years ago, I had a part-time job in a special school where there were a bunch of kids like Jacob. I grew fond of some of them. As a rule, they're sunny children. And there's no war in them."

He paused. Paul felt obliged to speak, although he hadn't understood most of his grandfather's words.

"Is he a monster?" he asked.

"Paul. You said the first thing that came into your head," his grandfather said.

"Does he look like a baby?" Paul asked.

"He looks like and is a baby. His eyes are a bit different from yours. Because his lids fold so"—Grandpa put a finger at the outer corner of each of his eyes and pulled slightly. "But he'll see out of them just as you see out of your eyes."

"When I was a baby, I wasn't different," Paul observed.

"That's nothing to brag about," his grandfather said. "All babies, especially those like Jacob, need a great deal of help. As time goes by, you'll probably think he's getting much more attention than you are. You'll be right. It can't be any other way."

"Is Daddy going to stop being an animal doctor? What will happen to Mom's students? Will I stay home from school?" Paul's questions tumbled out of his mouth.

"Yes and no," Grandpa replied. "Daddy will keep on working at the animal clinic, and you'll go to nursery school. But for a while, your mother will stop teaching piano."

Paul glanced over at the grand piano. It resembled a large mammal grazing on the rug. He had just learned about mammals from a picture book in school, and he imagined he could see them everywhere.

There were six children who came once a week for their lessons. They were well behaved except for Leopold, who was ten. He spent his hour half on and half off the piano bench, his feet pointed in the direction of the front door.

Paul finished setting up the checkers for another game. Mom, carrying Jacob, who was asleep again, followed by Daddy, returned to the living room. She lay the baby on the sofa.

Paul got up from his chair and walked across the room to stare down at Jacob.

His face was a round blob, like most infant faces Paul had seen. He reached toward the blanket to lift it and see if Jacob had a chin and mouth like everyone else.

"Don't!" his mother whispered. "You'll wake him."

"I'm hungry," Paul said.

The three people who always heard him were not listening. They were looking at Jacob.

"I'm hungry!" Paul repeated, more loudly.

"You ate breakfast an hour ago," Grandpa said.

"Have an apple," his father said.

"Now we have to settle him in," said Mom. The new him. He'd sleep in Paul's old crib with the white paint peeling on its bars.

She picked Jacob up from the sofa. The two men drifted behind her into the bedroom.

Paul backed to the piano, dropped to the floor, and crawled beneath it. He crossed his legs, let his head droop, and waited for Daddy to come and get him as he always had, laughing as he straightened Paul's legs, dragging him out by them until Paul began to laugh with him.

Daddy didn't come.

Paul could hear the three of them talking about groceries for lunch and supper, about a broken shade at the bedroom window, about *him*.

There were sudden piercing cries.

"Oh!" cried his mother. "He's awake!" exclaimed his father. "What lungs!" said Grandpa.

Paul clapped his hands over his ears. When he took them away a moment later, the living room was silent, the bedroom door closed again.

He crawled out from under the piano. The grown-ups had flown away like the pigeons that Paul chased in the neighborhood park when Mom wasn't watching him.

The small blue blanket lay on the floor where Mom had dropped it. He felt alone in the apartment for the first time in his life. It was too big. He crawled back under the piano to wait for someone to come. Grandpa walked out of the bedroom.

"Don't disappear into your piano house," he said. He sat down in an armchair. "Come here and sit on my lap." Paul was aware it was not a usual request. But he went to him and got up onto his lap. After a moment he rested his head against Grandpa's chest.

"I don't like him a lot," he said.

"You don't know him yet. There are four of you now. That's a big change. After a while you won't notice it so much. It will seem everyday."

Paul burst out, "But he's different!"

"Yes," Grandpa agreed. "And the difference will slip into your life like a flat stone into water, and you won't notice that either."

"I'm noticing it," Paul said.

Grandpa smiled. "I have to go pretty soon. Lindy will be missing me."

"Lindy is only a cat," Paul said.

"I'm only a grandpa; you're only a boy. Lindy doesn't know about such things. He'll be waiting for his midday snack. What he does know is what time it is."

Daddy and Mom came into the living room.

"I've missed you," Mom said, smiling at Paul.

"He's been such a good kid while you were at the hospital," Daddy said.

His parents and Grandpa filled up the room that had been so empty only a few minutes ago. It might turn out to be like any other day. But he knew it wouldn't.

"He can't play with my toys," he said positively.

"Oh, Paul!" his mother reproached him.

Grandpa lifted him from his lap and set him down on the floor. "You can play with my toys," he said.

Paul imagined the glass whatnot cabinet in Grandpa's studio apartment. On each shelf sat tiny baskets and crates and pottery containers of fruit and vegetables and fish. There were also bird nests of real straw upon which birds sat. Three of these could fit into Paul's hand. He had not been allowed to handle them, only look when Grandpa held them out to him. The nests and baskets and pottery containers came from all over the world, from places where

Grandpa had gone on his travels after Grandma died, before Paul was born. Italy and France, Burma and Japan and Mexico.

Whenever he went to visit Grandpa, the first thing Paul said was, "Can I look at your collection?" Grandpa would open the glass door and take things out, one by one, to show him.

Grandpa now rose from the chair. "You mean I'm old enough?" Paul asked.

"Yes. You're old enough," Grandpa said. He put on his tweed cap and headed for the front door. "I'll be going," he said.

Paul visualized Grandpa walking down the silent hall to the elevator. A block away he would drop into a subway hole. When a train pulled up to the platform, Grandpa would get on it, and emerge ten minutes later a two-block walk from his studio on the west side of the city. Paul had often taken that ride. Grandpa always took him to the lead car, where he pressed himself against a window and felt himself fly through the black tunnel that would explode into the yellow lights of stations.

"Come and talk to me," his mother said.

Paul walked toward his mother but halted a few feet away from her.

She held out her arms. When he didn't move toward her, she went to him and stooped and hugged him.

Inside her circling arms, a strand of her hair touched his face.

Paul told himself the story about how things had been before that morning, how Mom and Daddy leaned over his bed at night while he grew sleepier and dreamier, the sight of their faces all that he needed to carry him into the warm dark.

There was a cry from their bedroom. Mom released him and said, "Jacob is awake."

BIRTHDAY PARTIES

Although Grandpa didn't live far away and visited the Coleman family often, he wrote to Paul once a month, as he had since Paul was three. Mom or Daddy read the letters aloud to him, and they were like short stories from a book that didn't end.

There was often a sentence about Lindy the cat; how he had run up the synthetic curtain that covered the one large window in Grandpa's studio, and pulled threads from it with his claws; how he'd pinched a lamb chop from the stove when Grandpa wasn't looking, and right after he'd cooked it to his taste;

how he'd pounced on Grandpa from behind a door and clung to his trousers for at least a minute, and how Grandpa walked about the room, Lindy riding on his leg.

Paul kept all of the letters in a special box that resembled a large book. He had two favorites that Mom read to him frequently. One said:

"I was walking along West Street, thinking about one thing or another, breathing the smoky air that smelled of river water, when I saw a huge crab moving slowly across the sidewalk. What was such a creature doing in the big city? I could think of one answer, although there may be others. The crab must have come to town on one of the trucks that bring food to this city, probably coming from Chesapeake Bay, which runs along the shores of eastern Maryland and Virginia. It had managed to escape whatever container it was in, drop off the end of the truck, and here it was, skittering sideways in its crab fashion, trying, I guess, to find something familiar. I picked it up by one of its claws and walked toward the river. Most people didn't notice what I was carrying—or pretended they didn't. But one old man, who looked like me though much shorter and plumper, shouted, 'What are you doing with that crustacean! Put it down at once!' I walked past him as fast as I could. Fortunately, he didn't follow me. When I reached a pier that makes its ramshackle way out over the Hudson River, I dropped the crab into the water. It disappeared. I hope it's swimming back to the Chesapeake."

The other letter Paul liked to hear told of a new friendship.

"I've been buying my newspaper at a newsstand down the block from my studio apartment. Several weeks ago I found a new man behind the counter. His skin is like the dark Greek honey you're so fond of. His brown eyes gleam when he smiles. He has a musical voice and a fine mustache. His name is Nawaz. At first we just said good morning, then we began to talk a bit about the weather and the traffic jams. Very soon we were telling each other about our lives. He was born in a city called Islamabad in Pakistan, and he discovered that seven brothers had preceded him. Imagine that! One day, when a cousin was helping him sort the Sunday newspapers, I invited him for a cup of coffee. He seemed delighted. We went to a very pleasant, quite dark, little Italian coffee shop where we spent about twenty minutes finding out about each other. Now I get up every morning thinking about Nawaz and what interesting things he will tell me when I buy the newspaper."

The odd thing was that Paul and his grandfather never spoke about the letters when they were together.

Paul didn't write back to Grandpa. That would have meant telling his mother and father what to put down. Most of what he wanted to say was about Jacob: how he grew bigger but didn't change much in other ways; how he bawled and howled and stuck out his large tongue that was like bubble gum; how he didn't know one thing about playing with Paul; how Mom didn't play the piano in the evenings after supper because the sound would wake Jacob; how they were always taking him to doctors, and how Paul had to go along and sit in some office, waiting for days it seemed, staring down at torn magazines on his lap.

But he wrote letters in his mind, and by the time he was in the third grade, and Jacob had learned to stand up and walk, even to say some words, Paul could actually have written to Grandpa. By then, though, he didn't want to write a word about Jacob.

All the time he was learning to read and write, he had been teaching himself not to think about Jacob. That was simple when he went off to school, or visited a friend, or went somewhere with Grandpa. But it was hard when he was at home and Jacob popped up like a jack-in-the-box everywhere he went in the apartment.

It had been especially hard on Paul's eighth birthday party. Early that afternoon the tail end of a September hurricane had struck the city. The sky seethed with black clouds. Gusts of wind and fierce rain rattled apartment windows. Not one of the six school friends he'd invited came. Not even Grandpa turned up. The building's electrical power failed, and the day grew as dark as night.

But Jacob had screeched and laughed and clapped his fat hands as though the noisy storm was a celebration of something about himself. For the first time in Paul's memory, his mother had asked him to "keep an eye on Jacob," while she and his father put masking tape on all the windows so that if the glass broke, the fragments would stick to the tape. It didn't take them more than forty-five minutes, but Paul thought he'd go crazy with Jacob babbling and singing in some language of his own. It was almost as if the two of them were alone in the apartment and Jacob was a kind of human storm breaking around Paul, thundering and blowing.

The wind died down. The rain lessened. Lights came on. The storm was blowing out to sea. It was too late for birthday guests to come. His mother sat down on the couch and looked at Paul with a sympathetic smile. ". . . on your birthday," she had murmured.

Daddy said, "We'll have it tomorrow."

Paul shook his head. "I don't want any more parties," he said.

He saw them glance at each other. His mother said, "Perhaps you'll change your mind later."

He shook his head wordlessly.

"Well, we can eat the cake, although I expect the ice cream's melted because the electricity was off for a while. Then we'll open your presents—the ones we got you," his father said.

Paul said, "I don't want cake right now." Jacob was half asleep in the chair he'd climbed into. Paul felt far away from the three of them, as if he were looking at the living room where they sat through the wrong end of a telescope. But the distance frightened him a little, and so when his father said that at least he could *look* at the presents, he had quickly agreed.

One afternoon months later, after Paul had dropped his book bag on the living room floor and was heading for the kitchen to get an orange and a cookie, Jacob suddenly appeared from behind the sofa. He ran to Paul in his stumbling, rag-doll way and threw his arms around Paul's waist, pushing his head into Paul's stomach.

"Paul! Paul!" he cried. Paul froze.

"He loves you," Mom said from her bedroom doorway.

Paul didn't want Jacob to love him.

When Daddy told him they were going to have a little party to celebrate Jacob's fourth birthday, all Paul could think about was how he'd like to be somewhere else.

"We couldn't have a birthday party for him until this year," Daddy said. "The first three wouldn't have meant a thing to him."

If his father had known what Paul was thinking about, he wouldn't have sounded so calm. Paul was imagining an earthquake, a late spring blizzard, a fire in the apartment house—anything so long as he didn't have to be there when Jacob joined in with Mom and Daddy and Grandpa to sing happy birthday to himself in his crazy up-and-down shouting voice.

The day came. Jacob, wearing a wool cap embroidered with yellow rabbits that Grandpa had given him and that he wore at night in bed, was laughing, running, and falling all over the living room. Paul went to his room and lay down on his bed and tried to think about nothing at all. How could you think about nothing anyhow?

He felt pitiful, like an orphan left out of doors in the wind and the rain.

He heard paper being ripped. Shouts. He heard Grandpa saying, "This boy understands an occasion!"

"Paul," his mother called. "Jacob is opening the present you gave him. Come!"

He hadn't gotten a present for Jacob. They had. He didn't even know what it was. They had written his name on a birthday card.

"Paul!" cried Jacob. "My game!"

Grandpa appeared in Paul's doorway. "Do come along," he urged. "You'll feel better."

He got up slowly and went into the living room. How did anyone know how he was going to feel?

Jacob was sitting on the floor clutching an object constructed of heavy wires strung with brightly colored wooden beads. He looked up at Paul and let go of the toy. "Paul!" he shouted. "Thank you!" Paul couldn't help but notice Jacob's fifth fingers. They were like thick, short pencil stubs.

"You're welcome," he heard himself say in a thin, reedy voice.

Later there was a cake Mom set down on a low table. Jacob exclaimed, "Oh!" and at once thrust his hands into it, then his face.

"Gross!" Paul cried as Jacob grinned at him through globs of chocolate icing.

"You must never say such a thing to your brother," Daddy said sternly.

"I say it to my friends," Paul said defensively, his face hot.

"Jacob is your brother, not your friend," Daddy said.

Mom was looking at him with silent reproach. He much preferred Daddy's severe tone of voice to her expression, which clung to him like a damp cloth.

Jacob got sleepy at that exact moment. His head lolled and his mouth hung open. Mom took him to the bedroom, where Paul's old crib had been replaced by a small daybed. Jacob tumbled heavily from her arms onto the coverlet, which he burrowed beneath like some small forest creature.

Daddy was cleaning up the mess Jacob had made with his birthday cake. Grandpa said, "Let's go to the Museum of Natural History," and Paul ran to get his jacket, relieved. He was glad to leave the apartment.

At the museum Grandpa waited while Paul stared at the towering animals that had roamed through the landscape millions of years ago.

Grandpa seemed to have something in mind. As soon as Paul had finished with the dinosaurs, Grandpa led him through a huge hall where elephants paraded, their trunks flung up toward the ornate ceilings, their trumpeting stilled forever, as if they had met up with a magician and he had turned them into dark gray stone.

"Here!" Grandpa said.

Paul looked up at an illuminated circle inside of which, floating in somewhat clouded water, were leaves and branches and twigs and insectlike shapes.

"That's an inch of pond water magnified hundreds of times. Look at my hand." Grandpa formed a circle with his index finger and his thumb. "That's an inch," he said. "And that"—he gestured to the exhibit—"is what you see when you look at the inch through a microscope."

"It's like a whole little pond . . . a whole little neighborhood," Paul said.

"Worlds within worlds," remarked Grandpa. "The more you look, the more you see."

"Maybe if you magnified one of those twigs, you'd find a whole tree and lots of bugs," Paul said.

"I think so," Grandpa said.

When Paul was lying in his bed that night, thinking over the day, he recollected two things especially.

One was the magnified inch of pond water. After staring at it, he'd found mystery in everything he looked at: the birds flying over Central Park across the street from the museum, human faces, the blossoms on trees.

But after a while that wore off, and he was left with the second thing, which was that he'd gotten caught somehow when he said *gross* about Jacob trying to climb into his birthday cake. It wasn't only that Daddy had spoken so sharply to him. Paul had forgotten for a moment that he was learning to forget about Jacob.

MOVING

Mrs. Coleman had resumed teaching piano two afternoons a week. During those hours Josh, a thickly bearded, scraggly haired college sophomore, came to the apartment to watch over Jacob.

Josh was short and thin. When he ran into Paul in the apartment, he'd say, "Hi, man!"

It was as if a small animal, a badger or a beaver, peered out of a thicket to greet him.

In fair weather Josh took Jacob to a neighborhood playground. If the weather was bad, Josh read stories to Jacob in Paul's room, or read his own textbooks while Jacob stabbed at a piece of paper with a crayon or sang to himself.

Josh looked like a tired long-distance runner. Mom said it was because Josh had several part-time jobs to help with his college tuition.

Paul didn't like him. When he'd showed up on that first afternoon, Paul had warned him not to let Jacob touch anything in his room.

Josh said, "Wow, man! You sound like that's a law written before the Pilgrims landed at Plymouth Rock! But I know how you feel. I've got a younger brother who's always getting into my stuff and driving me nuts!"

Josh couldn't ever know how Paul felt. Jacob was not simply a younger brother. He wasn't made right.

Sometimes Gloria, a physical therapist who was supposed to help Jacob with his coordination, bounced through the apartment door like a beach ball and kissed Jacob on the top of his shaggy head. Jacob laughed until he fell down—of course, he was easy to please. You could show him an egg and he'd caper about like a clumsy kangaroo.

Would Jacob ever be able to do anything by himself? Why couldn't he learn things?

These were private questions Paul asked himself.

To his dismay, he found himself asking them of Dr. Newman, a counselor the Coleman family went to see from time to time after Jacob was born.

Daddy had said, "Perhaps you'd like to talk to Dr. Newman by yourself?" Mom had risen from her chair like a Roman candle, and the two of them had hurried out of the doctor's office, leaving Paul to sit mutely on a plastic-covered seat. In the silence that followed their departure, Dr. Newman looked at him genially, a faint smile on her lips. He shifted his glance away from her—how could his glance *weigh* so much?—to a boring painting of a mountain range on the wall behind her desk.

Suddenly he blurted out the questions that had been secret until that moment. He was mortified by the sound of his own voice, braying with complaint.

"He is learning all the time," she told him. "Your mother is a piano teacher, so you know something about tempo. Jacob's tempo is different from yours, slower. But it's still tempo."

He stared at her long, scarlet-painted nails, wondering how she held a toothbrush or picked up pieces of toast.

Another time, in the presence of his parents, Dr. Newman told Paul that he was the most important person in Jacob's life. Her words stuck like thorns in Paul's skull right up to the moment he had to stop repeating them to himself so that he could do his arithmetic homework.

There were moments when Paul imagined that Jacob was a star like the sun. He and Daddy and Mom, Jacob's dentist and baby-sitters—even Grandpa—and all the doctors who tended to his ailments were little planets forever circling him.

One afternoon Paul came home quite late after a visit to a school friend.

He discovered Jacob in his room, alone and sitting on the old rag rug like a big booby. Paul's books and games and toys, even his clothes, were scattered everywhere, as though a tornado had blown in through the window.

Paul couldn't help it. When Jacob turned to him smiling and calling out his name, Paul roared in a voice like a lion's, "I hate you! You dummy! Dummy! Dummy!"

Mom ran into the room, followed by Daddy, who had just come home and had not had time to take off his coat. They were both shouting.

"Paul! Wait!"

"Don't!"

"Stop!"

Jacob was weeping. Mom told Paul to go to his own room at once.

"I *am* in my room," he cried, his voice trembling.

They looked crazy. Jacob had driven them crazy.

"Jacob's got to have his own room. We've got to have more space," his father said grimly.

Paul had overheard them talking about more space for months. He had gone with them three or four times to look for it when he wasn't doing something with Grandpa. He had breathed in the air of "more space," dusty rooms that smelled of old carpeting.

But everything was too expensive. They couldn't afford to buy an apartment, and rentals were too high. Paul couldn't take it all in. Home was home. One day, it wasn't home anymore.

Daddy found a veterinary practice in a small town on Long Island called Brasston. It was fifty-eight minutes by train when the trains met their schedules. The Colemans planned to move at the end of June, after Paul completed fifth grade at the public school in the neighborhood.

When he thought about all the children in his classroom, when he imagined some of them looking at the teacher or the blackboard behind her or the big face of the clock on the wall, or staring out the grimy windows at the grimy windows of a building across the street, he felt only that he would miss the familiar surroundings of the school itself. But when he drew close in his imagining to a few faces that he knew so well, children he'd known from the first day he'd walked into the school six years earlier, his heart gripped inside his chest.

He made promises to those few that he would come into the city in the early fall, the first few days of September before school began. He would visit them then. But he knew somehow that it was unlikely he'd ever see those friends again.

"Tell me about your new house," Grandpa asked him at the beginning of their last week in the apartment. It had begun to resemble all the other empty two-bedroom apartments in the city.

Grandpa was leaning against Paul's bureau drawers, watching him pack his things into two big cardboard boxes.

"It's just a house. You can walk outside. No elevators," answered Paul.

"Isn't there anything agreeable about it?" Grandpa urged him.

Paul thought. "The landing," he replied after a minute. "The stairs turn around after they leave the second floor. Where they turn, there's a kind of platform and a round window with some colored glass panes."

"What about your room?"

"It's okay," Paul said. "There's a big yard with trees and bushes, and a leaky birdbath Daddy is going to patch up. My room looks out on it."

"How about the kitchen? Big enough to eat in?"

"There's a dining room," Paul said.

"Jacob will have his own bedroom now," Grandpa said reflectively.

Paul didn't comment. Why was Grandpa asking him about the house when he must have heard it described by Mom or Daddy?

As though he'd listened in on Paul's thought, Grandpa said, "I wanted to get your view."

"I like the veterinary hospital where Daddy is going to work," Paul said. "He told me it was a farmhouse long ago. There are woods across a big meadow, and a parking place for people underneath a horse chestnut tree."

"It will be a big change," observed Grandpa.

"It's all because Jacob needs more space," Paul said.

"You all need more space," Grandpa said.

Even with Grandpa, Paul felt a kind of thickening in his throat when Jacob was mentioned. He coughed.

"Have a sour ball," Grandpa said, handing him a green candy.

It was true that Paul got better at not thinking about Jacob month by month. But he discovered that he had learned to tell when Mom or Daddy or Grandpa wanted him to think about Jacob. He hadn't planned on that.

Kind thoughts, he remarked to himself sarcastically.

He sucked on the sour ball a moment. Then, after he'd wondered about how much more he could stuff into the carton, and had managed to slide still another book into it, he asked a question that had been much on his mind.

"How will I get to see you, Grandpa?"

"I like train travel," Grandpa replied. "It's a pleasant ride to Brasston if the train is on time. Your daddy informs me there's a small room on the first floor of your house where you can stick a cot so that I can sleep over. I'll bring Lindy, of course, in his cat carrier. Later on you'll be able to come into the city and visit me on your own."

"Will you write to me?" Paul asked. He'd noticed Grandpa's letters weren't half as frequent as they had been.

Grandpa held out his hands, stretching his fingers. "I have arthritis," he said.

Paul touched the knuckle of a swollen thumb. "Is that arthritis?" he asked.

Grandpa nodded.

"Does it hurt?" he said.

"It does, but it goes away from time to time. Rain and humidity bring it back. I don't think about it unless I have to pick up cuff links from the floor— then they slip through my fingers—or write letters. Anyhow, you're ten going on eleven. We can have long telephone conversations now."

Paul shivered although the air was full of June warmth. New house, new school, new place, and a new thought: Grandpa wasn't simply old. He was getting older every day, every minute of the day.

He realized that he was staring at Grandpa, and that Grandpa was offering his face to be looked at, as if it were a bouquet he was holding out to Paul.

His thick gray hair was cut short. His brown eyes sat in nests of wrinkles. He was tall and thin. His cheeks and chin were closely shaven, and the skin glistened.

"I've still got all my own teeth," Grandpa said, smiling.

Paul smiled back. There was a thought between them that Paul couldn't find a word for, a thought that emitted a faint buzz, like a sun-drunk fly.

Their smiles weren't about something comic but something sad.

Jacob began to cry in the living room.

"He's lost his eyeglasses again," Paul commented.

"Let's go help him find them," Grandpa said, walking to the door.

"I haven't finished packing," Paul said.

"Do you always know what he's crying about?" asked Grandpa, pausing in the doorway.

Paul shook his head in a way that didn't mean one thing or another.

Grandpa left, and a moment later the crying ceased.

In the silence that followed, Paul found himself trying to pack a soccer ball into a stuffed carton. A thought slid into his mind.

Was *not* thinking about Jacob only another way

of thinking about him? Before he could grasp the question's meaning, it vanished.

He suddenly recalled a day when he'd gone to Central Park with Grandpa. He had asked Grandpa to wait a few yards from the entrance to a dark tunnel they were passing. Then he had entered it, running.

At first he couldn't make out the words and sketchy drawings spray-painted on the tunnel walls. A dank moldy smell filled up the place like thick smoke. He had been excited by his own nerve, but it collapsed into panic several feet from the tunnel's exit. Later, when he and Grandpa went to the Central Park Zoo, he'd felt as if he were still running, as if pursued by the cruel, white glow of those words and drawings spray-painted on the walls of the tunnel.

BRASSTON

In the way that grown-ups make things happen, and a boy finds himself in a new place, a few days later Paul was unpacking books and games from a carton in a room that didn't feel like anybody's yet.

After the movers left, and Daddy and Mom were standing in the living room staring at the piled-up crates and boxes as though it were some gruesome Christmas morning, Paul walked out the kitchen door into the yard.

A dog barked from a nearby house. The motionless leaves of trees he didn't know the names of glittered in the early July sunlight. The weedy grass was high.

Being able to walk outdoors into the air didn't make up for school friends Paul would never see again. But it was something. Three steps and you were outside.

Gradually, over the next two months, the house became the Colemans' home. Books, rugs, vases, music scores, mirrors, furniture all made their appearance; they warmed up the boxlike rooms, made them familiar.

If Daddy wasn't obliged to go to the animal hospital on Saturdays, they took a picnic lunch to the ocean beach. Paul loved the south shore, its greenish sea, and the cold foaming water hitting his ankles. But he didn't care for these outings.

Jacob went off like a rocket the second he felt warm sand beneath his bare toes. He shouted and laughed in his husky burbling voice until everyone was staring at him, even the people who had their radios playing on the edge of their beach towels, next to their heads.

Paul would amble off down the beach, although he wasn't allowed to go into the water when he was out of sight of his parents. He couldn't really see why not. He was almost eleven.

These walks exhilarated him. He felt that nothing and no one stood between himself and the air, the brilliant sky, the seagulls plummeting toward the shore or the water, or floating on the wind. There were times when, after he'd looked about himself and seen he was alone, he'd shout in some incomprehensible, joyful language of his own invention, into the waves, into the breeze that blew off them.

He preferred to go alone, too, on the seven-block walk to Brasston's main street and shopping center. It was in the opposite direction from the public school he would go to in September.

There were small stores and eating places, a yellow-brick library where he applied for and received a library card, and a boarded-up movie house with letters missing from its marquee, so it read AL BAB AND THE 4 THIEVES.

What Paul liked most of all was going in the car with his father to the animal hospital. Then he could go on to the woods across the long meadow.

Dr. Gold, one of the other veterinarians who practiced at the clinic, told Paul it was one of the few patches of real forest left on Long Island.

"Every other place has been sold off for shopping malls or for housing like the development on the other side of the woods," Dr. Gold said. "Now don't you wander too far," the vet advised him, stroking a young cat that was hissing at him softly from an examining table. "Hush, Letitia! The worst is over," Dr. Gold murmured.

Paul paused by his father's office, and Daddy, without looking up, his attention on the medical records he was reading, said, "Be sure to be back in three hours, Paul."

He made his way across the meadow. It was filled with bramble bushes and overgrown weeds, some of which bore the tiny buds of unopened wildflowers. When he entered the woods, the strong summer sunlight broke, like thin plate glass, into glittering bits that fell upon leaves and protruding roots and tree trunks.

Paul heard a distant beelike drone of traffic from one of the highways that wound around and through Long Island. Now and then the sound of a chain saw, with its alligator jaws grinding noisily, reminded him of the housing development Dr. Gold had mentioned, which lay on the far side of the woods.

Birds he couldn't see would twitter along the boughs above him. Their shadowy movement among the leaves were like thoughts he couldn't quite catch hold of.

As he advanced further among the trees, the silence deepened. An agreeable touch of fear rippled down his arms. He was alone in a way that was different from being alone in his own room with the door shut.

Jacob would not come to these woods.

He found things. One afternoon, where the underbrush was thick, he reached out toward a large round stone to support himself. A minute later he had cleared away the brush from a crumbling stone wall. And a few yards farther on he discovered the shallow foundation of what might once have been a cabin or a small farmhouse. Nearby he found weathered wooden planks of various lengths strewn about the ground.

Without any plan, with the pleasure he found in being busy in these woods that he had come to feel belonged to him, he gathered all the lumber he could find. He came across a man's boot one day, and later on found its mate. He collected a pair of dirt-stiffened work gloves, a broken picture frame, a spool of rusted wire, and splintered pieces of a bamboo fishing rod.

He was careful to leave the woods in three hours, or in one or two hours—whatever Daddy had told him. He didn't want his father to come looking for him. He was always standing at the side of their car, a secondhand Camry that Dr. Coleman had had to buy at the end of their first week in Brasston.

"How was it?" Daddy asked one day as he started up the car.

"Okay," Paul replied.

"You'll meet other kids as soon as school starts," Daddy said.

"Yeah. I know," Paul said.

"I hope it isn't too lonely for you these days," his father said.

"I'm fine," Paul said.

He was full of the time he had spent in the woods, and as they drove along the quiet suburban street, he was happy. He had begun to make a clearing near the house foundation he had discovered.

"A woman brought in a sick parrot today. It has learned to say, 'Mummy! The phone is ringing!'" Daddy told him.

They both laughed. It was like the days before Jacob had been born, when Daddy came home with comic tales about the animal patients he had seen that day.

At home, on the kitchen table, there were baskets of peaches Mom had bought at a fruit-and-vegetable stand, and their fragrance filled all the rooms.

Paul ran upstairs. As he paused by the window that gave onto the yard, he saw Jacob's small trampoline. He pulled down the shade until his room was in shadow.

It was late August by then. The leaves of trees had lost their green gleam and were covered with summer dust. The lawns in front of houses turned the color of straw, and the air felt used-up and stale.

On the first Saturday in September Grandpa, carrying Lindy in his cat carrier, came to Brasston for an overnight visit.

Before he arrived, Jacob placed a large cookie, which he had taken several bites from, on the small rickety table that stood next to the cot Grandpa would sleep on in the spare room on the first floor.

When Paul discovered it there—a "present" for Grandpa, he guessed—a look of theatrical disbelief came over his face, although he was alone in the room at the time. Later he threw the cookie into the garbage can in the kitchen, choosing a moment when Jacob was there and saw him do it.

"Naw!" Jacob cried, gesturing with his whole hand at the garbage can. "My cookie for Grandpa!"

"Oh!" Paul exclaimed innocently. "I'll get it," and he reached into the can and took out the cookie, which had broken into pieces by then and was sprinkled with the coffee grounds Mom had just that moment thrown away.

Before anyone could speak, Paul handed Jacob the pieces of cookie and left the kitchen, grinning covertly, his face averted from Mom's look of inquiry.

Taking the stairs three at a time, Paul paused on the landing, hearing his mother's reassuring murmur to Jacob, and he was suddenly overcome with a fit of crankiness. "Served him right," he muttered to himself.

By lunchtime and Grandpa's arrival on the noon train, Paul's mood had changed for the better. Lindy, a tall regal black cat, prowled around the dining table, where the family sat eating fresh corn, big summer tomatoes, and walnut-sized new potatoes bought at the same stand the peaches had come from. There was a clap of thunder, and sheets of rain spilled from the darkening sky.

Grandpa smiled at everyone sitting at the table and said, "It's cozy here, nice!"

Jacob was sitting on Mom's lap, dreamily eating a peach and making a mess of it, mumbling to himself.

"I noticed when the station taxi drove by the movie house, it said 'new owner' on the marquee,"

Grandpa said. "And they're showing an Italian movie, *La Strada*, which I saw years ago. I'd like to take Paul to see it on this rainy afternoon."

"It's too old for him," Daddy remarked.

"If it's in Italian, I won't know what's happening," Paul said.

"Well, you can read," Grandpa said. "There'll be translations in English written at the bottom of the screen. Anyhow, this isn't a movie where you need to know exactly what people are saying."

"I want to go!" Jacob wailed, dropping the half-eaten peach on Mom's denim skirt.

Grandpa got up and went to Jacob. He examined his face like a monkey father would, chittering and touching his skin as if he were grooming him, then he tweaked his nose.

Jacob laughed. "Do it again," he cried. Grandpa did it again, and Jacob fell back, giggling, into Mom's arms.

"Later I'll take you for a walk," Grandpa said to Jacob. "And I have a special story to tell you!"

Jacob sat up and smiled. "Grandpa has a story," he whispered.

Paul recognized a coaxing tone in Grandpa's voice. You would have to be stupid not to know what was going on! Grandpa had been begging Jacob not to cry or yell.

Paul didn't like Grandpa doing that. Reasons, like soldiers, grouped in his mind, ready to march on Grandpa, ready to correct him.

Grandpa bent to pick up the peach and handed it to Jacob.

"Pa. It's a pretty sad movie. I don't think Paul's ready for that yet," said Daddy.

Grandpa looked at Paul. "He knows about sad things," he said.

Something odd is happening, Paul thought to himself. Grandpa never opposed his parents, but he was doing it now. The outings he and Paul had gone on, the conversations they had had since Paul's earliest years, had been about things that lay beyond his parents' authority over him; they had been, like the inch of magnified pond water, part of a larger world.

Then his grandfather gave up with a shrug. "Well . . . if you'd rather we didn't go . . ."

"I want to see it," Paul said, as though he were making an announcement.

"Considering what he sees on television . . ." his mother murmured.

"Okay," Daddy said.

Grandpa telephoned the theater to find out what time the movie began. By the time they set out to walk the seven blocks to the main part of Brasston, the summer storm had abated. The rain had thinned to a sprinkle.

"*La Strada* means 'the road,'" Grandpa explained to him. "Not just any road. It's what actors and circus people mean when they speak about going on tour. They visit towns and cities and villages, and people gather and the troupes perform. This movie is about two people, a strongman and a little country girl whom he, in fact, buys from her family. Not that she isn't eager to go with him! And it tells of their adventures on the road."

Paul wasn't listening to him. He was brooding about the walk Grandpa had promised Jacob.

"Where are you going to take him?" he asked as they passed the yellow-brick library.

Grandpa didn't answer right away. They had reached the movie house by then, and he bought their tickets from an old woman sitting inside a glass booth.

Then Grandpa turned to Paul as they walked through the lobby. "You can come, too," he said, to Paul's surprise. "Jacob would like that."

"I don't want to go!" Paul burst out as they were walking past the elderly man who took their tickets. He gave them a startled look.

"All right," said Paul's grandfather amiably as they went down the aisle of the dim movie house. There were no more than a dozen people sitting in their seats. The heat of the day had gathered there, and the air smelled of rancid butter from popcorn, the empty containers of which rolled about on the floor, dislodged by Paul's and Grandpa's feet.

The projector light went on. Across the black screen appeared the words *La Strada*.

"It's not in color," Paul whispered.

"You won't notice soon," said Grandpa.

On their way home Paul and Grandpa passed a lemonade stand built of rough planks. Two empty Dixie cups cast their lengthening shadows on the wood. Behind the stand two little girls drooped, their chins supported by their hands, staring into the dark green silence of the street. Someone called to them from the window of a yellow house that sat on a slight rise behind them. "Mira! Kira! Time to close up business! Supper!"

Everything in the movie had been run-down and grim and gray. Paul glanced up at his grandfather's face. He looked grim and gray, too.

Thinking about the movie, Paul had the feeling he had heard and watched a sermon in church. His grandfather looked as if he felt obliged to explain the sermon.

In the valleys, on mountaintops, the strongman and the girl gave their performances. The strongman knelt on the ground, warning onlookers with delicate feelings to look away, as he prepared to burst the chain he had bound about his chest. The girl, made up to look like a clown, played a dented trumpet. She wore a small black derby hat perched on the top of her head. Her eyelashes were exaggerated with black pencil lines. Their home was a little curtained wagon hitched to a motorcycle. But the strongman abandoned her one bitter-cold day.

After a long time the man returned to the stony village where he had first seen the girl. She had returned, too, but only to die. The movie's last scene had been of the strongman clutching a chain-link fence and weeping. He was mourning the loss of her, and her love for him.

"How could she feel sorry for the strongman! He

looked like he'd kill horses if he got a chance. She was so dumb to love him, so stupid!" Paul cried out in the quiet street.

Grandpa sighed. Paul knew it was because Grandpa thought he had to tell Paul what the story in the movie was really about. Paul clenched his jaw with irritation. It was the first time he could recall that he had been cross with Grandpa.

"There's a pity in love," Grandpa said after a long silence. "I can't say more than that about it."

He sounded helpless. That was for the first time, too.

When they got home, Mom and Daddy, at the same moment, asked Paul how he'd liked the movie.

"I didn't like it," Paul replied, staring down at his sneakers.

He went directly to his room after supper. Grandpa had gone out with Jacob. They were taking their walk.

Paul raised the window shade on the backyard before he turned on the light in his room. The glass pane of the window reflected lights from other houses.

Unbidden by him, the girl from *La Strada* appeared to his mind's eye standing beneath the branches of a maple tree in the yard.

He had learned the name of the tree during the summer months. He had learned the names of flowers and shrubs and insects, too.

The girl's black pot of a hat was clapped onto her head. She was lifting the banged-up trumpet to her lips, about to play the sorrowful, wordless song that had wandered through the movie like a scrap of paper caught by the wind.

When the strongman abandoned her on the deserted mountain road on a freezing afternoon, he had returned in a few minutes and covered her with several rags. Paul wondered, Had his stone heart been touched?

Almost at once he turned his attention to thoughts of school: how he would walk into the sixth-grade classroom next Thursday, what clothes he would wear, what expression he would have on his face. He was, after all, a new boy in the neighborhood.

THE AUTOBIOGRAPHY

During the first term of the sixth grade, in November, Paul got into a fight with Robert Brown.

"How's the retard?" he called out to Paul on an iron-gray afternoon as classrooms emptied out.

Robert had been held back in the fifth grade. He wasn't able to answer any teacher's questions, and he constantly dropped his schoolbooks.

Paul had scuffled with him, although his heart wasn't in a fight. It was like battling with a scarecrow, rags for clothes and sticks for bones. But Robert suddenly bit him on his right ear, and it bled.

The school nurse exclaimed, "Oh, Paul! You must not fight. Still . . . that was so loyal of you. You're such a good brother."

How did she know he had a brother? Did the whole town know? He'd get rabies from the bite, he told himself.

"I'm sure Robert didn't know what he was saying," she said, her hand pressing a bandage against his ear.

But Robert did know! And his words lodged in Paul's heart like shards of glass. Paul suspected it was because something inside him agreed with Robert Brown. Jacob *was* a retard.

"The bleeding has stopped," she said.

He thanked her and left the little office. Outside in the hall his friend George McCormick lounged against a locker.

"You'll get rabies," George remarked, grinning.

"I know it," Paul said with a pained smile. Would it be because of the bite? Or because of Robert Brown's question? It was weird to hear George's remark when Paul had secretly said the same thing to himself in the nurse's office.

When he got home that afternoon, his mother was giving someone a piano lesson, and Molly, the young woman Mrs. Coleman had hired to watch over Jacob, was playing with him in the dining room.

Playing. What did that mean where Jacob was concerned? Making faces, Paul thought. Only Jacob didn't have to make a face; he already had a permanent crazy one.

Paul felt a pinch of shame for his thought. Quickly he went to the telephone in the kitchen, glad there was no one there to ask him about the small bandage on his ear. He dialed George's number and, when his friend answered, said "Hello," and hung up instantly, choking with laughter. George must be laughing, too. Paul let a moment pass, then called again. At the first ring the phone was picked up at the other end.

"What was the fight about?" George asked.

Paul hesitated. He heard George's breathing.

"My brother," he said at last.

George didn't ask any more questions. They went on to talk about many things: school and homework, teachers and other students, the coming holidays, and what each of them planned to do during those glorious days when school was closed.

Afterward Paul felt a vague uneasiness, as though he'd forgotten where he put something. He was suddenly furious at the lid of a jar of honey, which he couldn't turn. A thought flashed into his head: Why hadn't George asked more about the fight he'd had with Robert Brown? Paul went to the sink, turned on the hot water tap, and held the jar beneath it. In a moment he was able to turn the lid.

Paul would see Robert Brown now and then around the school. He'd grown immensely tall, and he shambled along the school halls and dropped into his desk seat as though he were his own laundry bag. The other children called him "mule train." He seemed to have forgotten Paul and the fight he had had with him on the cold ground of the school yard. One afternoon as Paul walked past Robert, who was slumped against the wall looking blank, he had to stifle an impulse to ask, "Who's the retard now?"

Something happened after the fight that, when Paul thought about it, puzzled him. He became ambitious; he wanted to excel, to win at everything—soccer games, quizzes, essays—to get the highest grades in his classes, in the whole school!

It was as though a wheel was racing inside himself. He had to match the inside speed with outer actions.

It was difficult at first, like struggling up a steep slope of a mountain. He slipped; he stumbled;

sometimes he fell. But he kept on struggling up until the mysterious languages of arithmetic and science yielded to him.

Sometimes his mother and father asked to see his written essays. "Very good!" they'd exclaim. But what they said had ceased to matter. The A mattered. The teacher's comment in red pencil mattered: *This is fine work.*

He became the captain of the school soccer team. Only once was he criticized by the coach, who said, "Hey! Paul! This is a team! You're not supposed to be playing alone!"

He wished now that he hadn't refused his mother's offer to teach him the piano when he was little and his mother had been so eager to give him lessons. He might have won at that, too.

A week before Christmas vacation began, Mr. Stang, the English teacher, gave an assignment to the sixth grade. "Write your autobiographies," he said.

That afternoon, after pressing down the catch on the inside of his door, Paul began the assignment. After thinking for a few minutes in the early darkness, he switched on his desk lamp. He wrote:

"I play in the woods on Saturdays when my father

works at the animal hospital, which is about 1½ miles from my house. He's a veterinarian. There's lumber and an old stone wall and stuff left over from when the woods were used like a dump. It's not a huge forest, but there are enough trees to make it private. Last Saturday I collected wood and fallen branches and some steel netting that may come in handy. It got too cold there so I left early. If it doesn't snow next weekend, I'll bring a hammer and saw and some nails for the wood.

"I'm four feet, nine inches tall. My hair is brown like my eyes. I have a mother and a father and a living grandfather. My mother gives piano lessons. It's noisy at home when I get there after school, so I thought I'd build a place of my own in the woods."

It was not true that it was noisy at home.

Mrs. Coleman had seven students. She had acquired them in the six months the family had lived in Brasston. They were all well behaved except for a young man with three gold rings in his left ear. He had a long, lank ponytail secured by a rubber band, and he showed off his arpeggios but didn't complete a single piece of music. He was much given to banging out chords on the keyboard. Another student was an elderly woman, Mrs. Brandy, who played whole sonatas sedately and badly, with a proud expression on her face. The other five who came for lessons were children of various ages. One was as young as six.

The next day Mr. Stang asked Paul to stay a few minutes after class.

"I like what you've written so far," he told him. "It's original and lively. But there ought to be more details about your family. What about your little brother? I'd like to see some snapshots. Where were you born? Where do your people come from? An autobiography is about your life, after all."

How did Mr. Stang know he had a brother? First there was Robert Brown, then the school nurse. Now his English teacher mentioned Jacob, though not by name. The news about Jacob had gotten around.

Paul felt a clutch of worry—what if Mr. Stang wrote *unsatisfactory* across that page he was waving so casually in the air?

"We all come from somewhere," Mr. Stang said pensively, staring past Paul at the big window in the classroom. "We all have a history."

When Paul got home that afternoon, Jacob seemed infected with giggles the way people are infected with cold symptoms. All through supper and after, the sound of it, like a small stream coursing over pebbles, filled up the house.

Dr. Coleman had brought home from the hospital an orphaned black kitten for Jacob.

Jacob lay down on the living room rug. The kitten jumped on his back and pawed his rag-doll hair. Jacob couldn't hold up his head because he was laughing so hard. Dr. Coleman and Mrs. Coleman smiled at him. As Jacob turned his face to the kitten's and tried to kiss him, they suddenly embraced as if they'd just discovered they loved each other more.

Paul had cleared the supper dishes from the table. He stood now in the dining room doorway and watched his family. He felt helpless. He couldn't speak. He was unable to make his presence known to them. He had become invisible.

Since Jacob's birth there had been other moments like this one, moments when Paul felt himself erased like a chalk boy on a blackboard.

Jacob simply was. There was no difference between his inside and his outside. If he belched, Mom and Daddy would look at him with concern written on their faces. If he cried, they flew toward him like swallows at twilight fly to the eaves of houses.

"You must name your kitten," Daddy said to Jacob.

The kitten squirmed and escaped from Jacob's awkward grip. It leaped across the living room floor, its paws touching the rug like a series of staccato notes played on the piano.

Jacob shouted, "Oh, cat!"

Paul started to walk across the living room to the stairs, already shaping his lips to say that he had homework—in case they asked him where he was going.

"His name is Paul!" Jacob cried.

"No!" exclaimed Paul.

He could not look at Jacob. He knew how stricken his expression would be.

"Perhaps, Jacob dear, we can think of another name for the kitten. How will Paul know if we're not calling *him*?" She laughed in a way that Paul knew was fake.

But Jacob appeared not to have heard Paul's *no*. "I call him Jack!" he said excitedly. "Jack and the beanstalk!"

"Wonderful," Mom said.

"Great," Daddy said.

Paul fled up the stairs and went to his room.

It was bad enough that Jacob had wanted to name the kitten Paul. But his mother's pretend laughter!

And Mom's "wonderful" and Daddy's "great" were forced out of them and hid the truth. They'd been relieved, that was all. A crisis had been avoided with Jacob. No scene; no tears.

It struck him suddenly that it was the way they spoke about Mrs. Brandy. Oh—she was so beautiful! So musical! She tries so hard despite her arthritis!

Yet he had noticed age spots all over her hands. He had seen the wrinkles around her eyes and mouth. She was losing her hair. She was going bald!

How they praised Jacob for the most ordinary things he did!

Paul knocked several books off his desk, feeling a remote pleasure in the way they smacked the floor. No one would come running upstairs to see if he'd fallen down.

A sense of desolation came over him; it was like the listless feeling he had on a cold Sunday when the chilly rain fell, and he was standing at a window, staring at the outside.

He had to write his autobiography again. He wrote: "My father's family came from Northern Ireland about one hundred years ago. My mother's ancestors had settled here a long time before that. They were Swedish—or Polish. I was born in New York City at Beth Israel Hospital."

They had brought him home in a taxicab. He'd been born in September. His mother hadn't been worried about him because, she said, he was a perfect baby.

He added a few sentences to what he'd already written.

"My brother, Jacob, has Down syndrome. He looks sort of Asian because of the way his eyelids fold. His teeth are small like the little fingers of his hands. He's going to be seven at the end of April."

Paul paused and stared up at the ceiling. He imagined that he saw there a large, blobby heart. Written inside it were his and his brother's names.

Jacob was best. It sounded like an oak tree or a lion. His own name was pale and watery.

"I'm the lion," he said aloud.

He looked over what he'd written. Then he added a sentence he'd heard recently. "We don't have much in common."

DR. COLEMAN'S REQUEST

On the evening of the day in April when Paul's father had run after him on the path that led from the house, seized him by his shoulders, and turned him around to face Jacob at the living room window, Paul heard through his closed bedroom door the notes of a guitar.

His father, who was playing it, began to sing in his high tenor voice,

"The fox went out on a chilly night,
  And he prayed to the moon to give him light . . ."

Jacob would be lying in his bed, his mouth gaping, looking as if he were hearing the song for the first time instead of the millionth time.

Daddy had played and sung the song for Paul when he was little, in his old bedroom in the New York City apartment, long before Jacob was born.

But Paul was beginning to think about Jacob. That had to stop.

He went back to work on a page of math problems. Soon he had blocked out the sound of Daddy's playing and singing. He didn't hear the knocking on his door for several moments, until it grew louder.

He got up, walked to the door, and unlocked it. His father came into his room and, after pushing aside a pile of books and discarded clothes from a chair, sat down.

"What are you doing?" his father asked, smiling at him.

"Math. Homework," Paul answered.

"You having any trouble with it?" Daddy asked lightly.

"No," Paul said, louder than he meant to.

"I didn't think so," Daddy commented. Then, after a silence, his father said, "You'll be twelve in September."

"Yes."

"I thought maybe you could help us in a different way from being a fine student and writing all those beautiful essays," Daddy said.

Paul looked at him warily.

"Jacob is going to attend a special school after his birthday at the end of this month." Daddy spoke formally, as though he were reading from a speech.

"There will be other children like him in the school. He'll learn lots of things. In that way, he'll be made ready for his life," he said.

Then he spoke with an emotion Paul didn't recognize. "That's what has frightened your mother and me so much . . . that he might not have a life when he grows up."

Dr. Coleman stared at the square of darkness that was the window. When he turned his head to face Paul, his eyes were wide, as though with strain.

"The people who run the school told us that people like Jacob can learn trades. He'll be able to support himself. He'll earn a real salary," he said.

"When does he start?" Paul asked.

"His seventh birthday is two weeks from this Sunday," Daddy said.

"I know," Paul said. "Will he be gone the whole day?"

His father's laughter startled him. "He is a pain in the neck, isn't he?"

It was the first time Paul could recall that Daddy had spoken about Jacob in such an ordinary, everyday sort of way.

But if he acted on his impulse and agreed with Daddy, it would mean that he was agreeing with everything his parents had said over the years about Jacob—that Jacob was only a small extra trouble, that they were an ordinary family.

Paul thought back on how the conversation about Jacob had started. "What am I supposed to do?" he asked resentfully.

"We'd like you to take him to Dr. Brill tomorrow morning for his allergy shot, and again next Saturday morning. He loves the walk there. You'll have to give yourself plenty of time. He dawdles. If you'll take him, it will leave your mother free to give Mrs. Brandy her lessons. She's had to cancel her regular appointments because of grandchildren visiting—"

"No!" Paul cried, interrupting.

His father's expression changed, hardened. He had sounded ever so faintly apologetic up until now.

He said in the rough voice that made Paul feel like nobody's child, "You have no choice in the matter!"

"But everyone will look at me!" Paul exclaimed.

"So what," Daddy said flatly.

"Kids will see me with him," Paul muttered.

"Everyone knows about Jacob," his father said.

Paul felt a shudder run through his entire body. He imagined all of Brasston knowing about Jacob; he thought of what George would say, George who said the worst, most comical things about the teachers, the kids in class, strangers on the sidewalks— things that made Paul double over with laughter.

His father picked up one of Paul's sneakers from the floor and began to turn it slowly in his hand.

"It will be different—if we're *seen* together," Paul said after a moment.

"Do you think other people have no troubles?" his father asked suddenly.

Paul didn't answer.

"We need your help. You can't go on forever as if you don't have a brother," his father said. He let the sneaker drop onto the floor.

George had a younger brother, Matthew. Paul thought of all the younger brothers and sisters he knew. Jacob was the only one among them who was unfinished.

"His appointment is at ten A.M. You'll need forty-five minutes, maybe an hour. He has a whole routine," Daddy said.

Paul hadn't known Mom was taking Jacob to Dr. Brill for allergy shots on Saturday mornings.

"Daddy," Paul began hopelessly. "Can't you take him? I really don't want to."

His father's face softened. "I know you don't want to do it," he said. "But I have to work at the hospital. There's something good about having a brother like Jacob, even though you won't understand it for a few years . . . when you're grown-up. People don't think about trouble until it slams into them. You'll be more ready for it. It always comes—in one form or another." He paused. "We weren't ready for it," he said carefully, as though choosing his words. "Jacob has been a test for Mom and me. One day we fail. The next day we get a B."

What Paul understood was that if he didn't give in, there'd be endless trouble. His parents would think of all sorts of things to take away from him, things he didn't even know he had. He'd be grounded; he'd lose telephone privileges; he wouldn't get his supper! But this last was too much of an exaggeration even for Paul.

The real consequence of his taking Jacob to Dr. Brill for his appointments would be that he wouldn't be able to practice not thinking about him. Jacob would haunt him all day long. Paul was being drawn into the life of his family. It felt like the inside of the school bus when it was filled with kids—warm, crowded, humid.

Saturdays had been lifted out of the week, taken away from him.

When his father got up to leave his bedroom, Paul said good-bye, instead of good night. When he thought about it later, when he recalled his father's momentary puzzlement, he realized it hadn't been a mistake. He had been saying good-bye to his old life . . . the old life of not thinking about Jacob.

Soon the house grew silent. Like an animal curling about itself, it settled down. Jacob was asleep in his room. Mom and Daddy were probably sitting at the kitchen table, probably talking about Paul in voices kept low so that he wouldn't hear them.

Paul went into the hall and to a small storage room where luggage was kept and winter clothes already hung in bags that smelled of moth crystals.

There were boxes of books the Colemans had not found space for, and odd bits of china and glassware. An exposed bulb dangled from the ceiling, and he turned it on.

He noticed a painting leaning against a wall, one he remembered from the apartment in New York City. It showed a house with a wide white porch. The house's shadow fell across a lawn that led to a brilliantly blue bay where tiny islands sat like puffs of smoke.

Paul used to pretend that he and Mom and Daddy were having a picnic on that lawn. It was July and sunny. Later they would swim in the bay. The long summer twilight would come like a light blanket pulled up to keep them warm against the cool night breezes.

In one of the boxes he discovered a thick photograph album, and he sat down on the dusty floor.

He began to turn the pages. There were snapshots of his parents, taken centuries ago, when they looked as young as teenagers.

Then he was born. The pages were filled with an explosion of photographs, some in penny-candy colors, the more formal ones in black and white. His history was recorded until he turned five. There were a few birthday snapshots of his fifth birthday party, the cake, the children of friendly neighbors in the building where he had lived in the city, the heap of unwrapped gifts. Then the pages were blank.

Paul turned them irritably, not knowing what he was searching for. There came a page with a single enlargement in color on it.

It was a picture of his mother emerging from a big building—the hospital, he guessed. She was carrying the new baby, Jacob, wrapped in a blue blanket. He was sleeping. She was trying to smile, but her eyes seemed to Paul to be sad, bewildered.

He turned the pages back until he found one of himself in the fork of a tree. It must have been taken in Central Park about the time he turned five. Jacob had been born by then. Daddy must have wanted to get away from the apartment and the baby, because he'd hurried off with Paul to the park.

Paul had been laughing when he peered through the branches at Daddy. He couldn't have understood the news Grandpa had given him about Jacob yet.

That his parents had stopped taking pictures was a sign to Paul of their discouragement over Jacob. No wonder they were discouraged, he thought.

He put the album back in the box, turned off the

light, and went into the hall. Jack the kitten was sleeping curled up in the center of a throw rug, a small circle of fur, the night-light in the baseboard glowing behind him.

The thought of tomorrow—the walk to Dr. Brill's office with Jacob stumbling, circling, clinging as he tried to wind himself around Paul—was worse than anything that had happened to him. There was no way out of it.

THE FIRST SATURDAY

While Jacob was being dressed, or dressing himself, or clothes were magically flying through the air toward him, Paul waited with grim patience on the sidewalk in front of the house. His hands were shoved into the pockets of a stained jacket, the sleeves of which left his wrist bones exposed.

He was wearing his oldest clothes and nothing quite fit him.

At his ordinary pace he could walk to the commercial area of Brasston in ten minutes. On his bicycle he could do it in two minutes. That was when he was alone, of course.

He heard the front door open and close. Jacob shrieked, "Paul!"

Paul turned involuntarily toward the house. His mother was standing on the front steps that led up to the door, holding Jacob's hand and smiling at Paul in a strained way. He knew she was acting as though his taking Jacob to the doctor was a normal sort of thing.

He didn't respond to Jacob's crying out his name. He averted his gaze and stared at a crack in the cement sidewalk. Two ants scurried along the crack. Paul imagined how the sides of it would appear to the ants, like cliffs towering above them. He recalled the magnified inch of pond water in the Museum of Natural History. He *was* thinking about something other than Jacob; he was comforted by that thought, and he felt a touch of triumph.

Jacob was dragging Mom down the small path that led from the house to the sidewalk. She cried, "Jacob! Jacob!" with sham merriment. Now he couldn't help but hear Jacob's excited breathing.

In a flash she had switched Jacob's hand to Paul's—and Paul had shaken himself free of it.

She cleared her throat as she went back up the

path to the front door of the house. Her head was bowed.

Paul's face was as empty of expression as a clam-shell.

But behind his face, his thoughts were scudding through his mind like clouds on a windy day. They were dark, thunder-filled thoughts, full of wordless resentment.

He took a step. Jacob took one, laughing, yipping like a puppy.

Paul began to walk quickly. Jacob had trouble keeping up with him. A couple came out of their house down the block. The man shouted after the two boys, "Taking your brother somewhere? That's nice. . . ." A dog standing on a recently sodded lawn looked at them distractedly and suddenly ran off, its collar tags chinking.

Onward they walked, Paul looking neither to his right nor his left, but moving forward in a straight line as though he were following a ruler edge. Jacob tried to keep up with him, watching his face for clues.

In the middle of the fourth block from the house, Jacob moaned once. Paul felt a trickle of uneasiness. Jacob ran into a hedge in the rush-and-tumble of his movements. He banged into tree trunks. He veered off the sidewalk into the frayed ropes of a swing someone had put up in the branches of an old oak. He blundered into recently raked and planted beds of earth. He left prints of his shoes in the damp April ground wherever he stumbled.

By the time they reached the commercial section of Brasston, Jacob was panting like a running dog. He couldn't speak, though Paul saw that he was bursting. His freckled skin was covered with beads of sweat.

Now there were people on the sidewalks. They emerged from the pizza parlor and the delicatessen, they lingered over the display of magazines and newspapers in front of the newsdealer's store, they sauntered from the Cards and Notions Shop, looking back at the display windows as though dimly regretting whatever it was they had bought.

Jacob and Paul arrived at the squat, stucco-covered Medical Arts building, around the corner from the movie house where, last September, Grandpa had taken Paul to see an Italian movie whose title he had forgotten.

They were thirty-five minutes early for Jacob's appointment with Dr. Brill.

Paul sat down on a beige couch across from where Jacob had sunk into a plastic chair as soon as they'd come into the waiting room. When Jacob caught his breath, he crossed over to the couch. He put one hand hesitantly on Paul's knee and smiled at him. Paul averted his face.

THE SECOND SATURDAY

Did Jacob have a memory? Would he recall last Saturday? The march to Dr. Brill's office? Would he be afraid of Paul's anger?

Paul, assailed by such questions, waited for Jacob in front of the Coleman house. A small ember of rage smoldered inside his heart simply because he was waiting.

But he was scared. He was dismayed and confused. He made a resolution to let Jacob take his time today. He had rushed Jacob to the doctor's at a cruel speed last Saturday, angrily. What if there was a total breakdown in Jacob's behavior today? What if Jacob hurtled through the front door of the house, red-eyed and gnashing his small teeth, heaving curses and rocks at Paul?

When Jacob appeared, he looked meek but determined. A knitted elfin cap sat on his head. Paul looked at it and was instantly irritated. Jacob wasn't eager or breathless with excitement; he didn't even glance at Paul. He sang to himself as he descended the three steps that joined the path to the sidewalk. His progress was wavering yet purposeful.

Jacob kept on going past Paul. He continued his tuneless singing. "I'll send cat Jack off to the kitty store with a kitty dollar. . . ."

As Paul reluctantly followed him, he saw how Jacob circled tree trunks he had crashed into last week. He saw how Jacob stared at the ropes of the swing hanging from an oak branch and went by them.

He avoided fresh beds of earth and the young, fragile shoots of ground covers.

When they reached the last block of the residential area of Brasston, they were far apart on the sidewalk. Each boy looked as if he were alone.

Jacob turned in unexpectedly at the newsdealer's store. The Pakistani owners greeted him with smiles.

They both looked over at Paul, who stood at the entrance to their store, frowning.

Paul suddenly thought of Nawaz, the Pakistani whom his grandfather had befriended. For a moment his face cleared. He smiled back at the older of the two men, whose gray hair made him think of Grandpa. But as the name of the day, and the name of his task—taking Jacob to Dr. Brie—came back to him, his expression grew stony. He stood with his hands in his pockets, staring down at the dusty, shel-lacked floor.

"You want a funny book, Jacob?" asked the gray-haired man.

Paul glimpsed Jacob nodding crazily so that his head appeared about to snap off his neck. The other man went to a bundle of tied-up comic books in the back of the store. Paul guessed they would give Jacob an out-of-date issue.

A moment later Jacob, holding the comic book aloft like a banner, marched out of the store. He went right by Paul as though he were by himself and on this spring morning had stopped by the news-dealer's on his way to see the doctor.

Paul was puzzled, exasperated, when Jacob went into the delicatessen next door. Paul sighed dramatically and followed him. Jacob went right to the deli display case and was greeted by the man on the other side of it, who was wearing a short chef's hat.

"Jakie!" exclaimed the counterman. "What can I do for you?"

At that instant a fat woman wearing a large white apron emerged from a swinging door behind the counter. She went right to Jacob and hugged him. "My little dumpling," she crooned as she gave him a piece of pastry. He stuffed it into his mouth the second she released him.

The counterman asked, "How's the boy?" before he turned back to whatever he was grilling. It was as though Jacob were all right.

His visits were not over. Next he went into the Cards and Notions Shop just beyond the delicatessen. Two young women were arranging displays for the morning's business.

"Little Jakie," said one. "How are you today?"

"Going to get your allergy medicine?" asked the other.

Jacob crowed like a rooster. But all the time he was looking at Paul, who had stayed at the entrance to the shop.

One of the young women gestured toward him. "Is that your older brother? Is he taking you to the doctor?"

Her hands were filled with elaborate birthday cards, which she was building into a pyramid on a display table.

Jacob said, "He's not my brother."

Paul agreed with him silently, but a second later felt so great a chagrin that when the woman laughed and said, "He is too your brother!" he felt an aggrieved vindication.

Jacob stared at her. He wasn't smiling; he wasn't bawling. He was just looking.

"He's watching over you," she added as she fiddled with the last card.

Jacob did something then. He took three steps to the table and knocked over the pyramid of birthday cards with an awkward slap of his hand.

"Oh! Jakie!" exclaimed the woman with exasperation, but a moment later she said, "Well—that's all right. I'll just do it again."

They were making allowances for his condition, Paul told himself. All these store owners were determined to stay good-humored no matter what Jacob did.

They left the Cards and Notions Shop and passed beneath the movie marquee. This Saturday Paul remembered the title of the Italian movie his grandfather had taken him to see last summer: *La Strada*. It had been an unpleasant experience for Paul, and, half an hour into the movie, he had stopped reading the English subtitles.

Jacob went up the walk to the yellow-brick library. For the first time that morning, his body sagged. His head was down. Paul, following a yard or so behind him, asked himself in annoyance what Jacob was up to now. He couldn't question Jacob; he'd promised himself not to.

This morning, which he'd been dreading all week, had come and was nearly gone. He would soon have done what he'd been asked to do—no more, no less.

Jacob had entered the library, and Paul hastily followed, wondering what on earth Jacob would find to do among all the books.

The librarian looked up from her circular desk and smiled. "Hello, Jacob," she said.

"Hello, Miss Greene," he replied. "Do you have a book for me today?"

"Yes," she said. "I had hoped to see you last Saturday. In fact, I kept this one for you."

She held out to him a copy of *Millions of Cats*.

Paul saw that Jacob was about to get into trouble because of the comic book he was gripping. He didn't seem to know what to do at first, whether to let go of the one so that he could take the other, or hold one in each hand. Then he held the comic book in his teeth and with his right hand took the book Miss Greene had saved for him. With his left, he searched a pocket in his jacket until he produced a library card. This he handed over to Miss Greene. She slipped it under the electronic camera and handed it back to him.

It was all pretend, judged Paul. Everyone was pretending Jacob was normal.

They stood at the top of the library steps several feet apart. Jacob carried *Millions of Cats* in one hand, the comic book in the other.

He suddenly began to weep.

It was at that moment that Paul saw George and his little brother, Matthew, looking up at them from the bottom of the steps.

Jacob was sobbing out loud. Paul felt stricken and angry at the same instant. He couldn't think of what to do to comfort him.

"Jacob, what's the matter?" George asked. He knew the name of Paul's brother!

"Oh, come on! Don't cry," George urged.

Jacob stumbled down the steps to him. When he was standing in front of George, his crying stopped. He was staring at the other boy's face, his cheeks wet with tears. He said "Paul" softly, turning his head to look at his brother.

"Did he do something to you?" George asked humorously. And he gave Jacob a pat on his head. Matthew was hopping up and down, first on one foot then on the other. "Hey, Paul!" George exclaimed. "What did you do to him?"

How had he discovered Jacob's name?

"Bye-bye," George said with a crinkling of his fingers and a grin. He and Matthew walked on.

Paul and Jacob were twelve minutes late for the appointment with Dr. Brill.

ESCAPE

It was the last day of April and Paul awoke early. The light was like a gray gauze adhering to everything he could see from his bed. Gradually a pale lemon light slipped under the gauze.

It was Jacob's birthday. The Colemans were having a party for him. Grandpa would be the only guest. He would arrive on the morning train bringing Lindy.

He had come to every one of Paul's birthdays as far back as Paul could remember, except the day of the hurricane's tail. Sometimes, as when they'd first moved to Brasston, he was the only guest.

Paul was going to the woods—*his* woods, as he thought of them. He'd take a sandwich, a can of soda.

He'd go early to escape the preparations for Jacob's birthday: the cake making, the snappers placed next to the place mats on the table, the balloons being blown up, the presents wrapped.

What could Jacob be given for his birthday?

It would hardly have meaning for him, this celebration of the day he'd been born. Except for the excitement of the occasion, there'd be no sense in Jacob of having lived another year, no feeling of accomplishment.

He lived in the present; he had no private life of thoughts and feelings; he had no secrets.

It was time for Paul to get up. He'd go to the kitchen, eat a bowl of cereal, make himself a sandwich, go out the back door with a casual air of being free.

Mom and Daddy would be busy. If he met either one of them in the kitchen, he wouldn't say where he was going—to his private forest to spend the hours of the day.

In the hustle and bustle of the birthday preparation, his leaving wouldn't be noticed.

He remembered his own fifth birthday a few months after Jacob had arrived from the hospital.

Paul had been told by Grandpa about Jacob's "condition" that first day Mom had carried the new baby into the living room of the apartment. A day or so later, Daddy and Mom spoke about it to Paul, but he'd barely listened. It hadn't meant much of anything to him then; a faint shadow of what it had come to mean to him.

Now, he tiptoed down the stairs, urgently wishing to avoid meeting anyone. But he found his mother in the kitchen, staring at the electric coffeepot wheezing on the counter.

"Happy birthday," she murmured to Paul without glancing at him. She turned to smile—at Jacob, he realized. He had caught the "Jacob smile" on her face before she'd replaced it with the "Oh—it's you" look.

But then she looked stricken, as though she'd suddenly recalled that it wasn't just anybody; it was Paul. He thought that was why she covered her mouth with her hand for a second; that was why she had flinched right after the "Jacob smile."

She turned back to the counter and the coffeepot, now done with its brewing. Her arms were folded across her chest; she appeared to be listening.

It reminded him of how she looked when she sat down at the piano, as if she listened for something.

It was just a moment, but until she heard that mysterious call—or note—from outer space or wherever, until she felt that beat, that tempo, she couldn't play music. It stirred him to imagine her like that, with a separate self, with work to do.

He thought of his own resolution about what he was planning to do that day, and he felt uneasy.

He realized he had dismissed Jacob's birthday, telling himself his absence wouldn't matter.

But he'd also told himself he need not bother to say where he was going.

He looked at her covertly. Then he took a banana from a bowl on the kitchen table and opened the junk drawer where, among other objects, old plastic bags were stored. He slipped one out, watching her all the while. But she didn't turn around.

He was able to put peanut butter on a piece of bread and fold it over, and to take from the refrigerator a bottle of orange soda before she startled him with a question:

"Where are you off to?" she asked. "Can I fix you some breakfast?"

"I'm going to meet George," he answered quickly.

"That's good," she said. "You can spend the morning with him. Jacob's party begins at one o'clock.

You can be back in plenty of time for that." She sighed then.

Paul poured himself a glass of milk. He hadn't answered her statement about being back in time for the party. He hadn't agreed or disagreed with it.

She poured herself a cup of coffee, which she always took black. It seemed to wake her up.

She began to move briskly around the kitchen, putting a glass of orange juice on the table for Jacob, a bowl for his cornflakes, a coffee cup for Daddy.

Paul was drinking the last of his milk. As the time of his departure grew closer, he began to feel anxious about it, as though something might prevent him from leaving.

"George will be waiting for me in front of the library," he told her unnecessarily. "I have to go."

"Did you get enough breakfast?" she asked him, a sudden worry making her frown.

He nodded, not sure she was looking at him and would catch the nod.

He went out the back door and into the yard. The gray he had woken up to had been swept away by a fresh-smelling breeze. Sunlight, the color of butter, lay in streaks across the ground; the matted grass, which Daddy had neglected last summer because of the pressure of his veterinary work, had a spongy feel to it.

Paul hauled his bicycle out of the garage, then wheeled it down the driveway to the street. He was free!

He sped like a messenger on his bicycle along the Brasston streets, although what message he'd been entrusted with, he didn't know. Something about freedom, something about getting away from Jacob, he guessed.

When he reached the old house in which the animal hospital had made its offices and consulting rooms, he avoided the parking lot beneath the horse chestnut tree. Dr. Gold might have come in for an emergency appointment.

He biked across the meadow slowly, pausing to remove clods of earth from the wheels, postponing the delight he would feel on entering the woods— so as to make the anticipated moment sweeter. When he was a few yards away, he got down from the bicycle and burst into a run, keeping a grip on the handlebars, yelling words of joy and deliverance.

GRANDPA

Paul, elated, thrashed among the branches that had fallen on the ground during the winter months. He laughed aloud; he sang a song of his own devising to himself. Then he remembered Jacob's kitty song, and he swallowed the last word of his song, which was *escaped*, and fell silent.

He was missing the birthday party. Grandpa would arrive cheerfully, his voice ringing with birthday wishes. What was there to wish for Jacob? It would be a mournful occasion; Jacob close to tears with excitement, the three grown-ups looking sad except when Jacob looked at their faces. They'd smile then, and coo at him.

It was the first time Paul had not been at one of Jacob's parties. In the New York apartment he'd been closed up with no place to go, and so he'd gone to sit at the birthday table, adorned with crepe paper, paper hats beside each plate. He'd been silent there, making hideous faces when attention was on his mother as she brought in the birthday cake or on Jacob as he shouted and wailed "Happy birthday!" to himself.

Paul's mood veered like a paper boat blown by the wind on the surface of a pond.

A long time ago, before the winter, he had been gathering supplies to build himself a shelter. Now he began to collect evergreen branches for a roof. But his feeling of freedom, of making choices, deserted him.

It seemed airless in the woods. He felt he was in a little child's drawing of a forest of crayon trees.

It was Sunday. The carpenters and masons and electricians who had been working on the houses at the far side of the woods, and whose voices Paul realized had been a comfort to him, were gone.

Time passed heavily. Paul sighed. There was

nothing to do in the woods today. Except eat lunch. He ate his sandwich, standing in a ray of sunlight that slipped through the boughs above him. He guessed it was about noon from the position of the sun.

Jacob's birthday party would begin soon. It would be over in an hour or so. His mother didn't want the excitement to exhaust Jacob for the rest of the day.

On Monday Paul's parents would accompany Jacob to his special school. They would do that for a week, then he'd take a small orange bus with EAGER TRANSPORT written in black letters across its side. Was Eager the name of the owner? Or did it mean that the company that owned the bus was eager to transport its damaged little passengers to school?

Everything was changing. All except Jacob. No matter what he learned in his special school, it wouldn't change him.

Paul heard a sound on this windless day. It was the noise of a shoe hitting a tree root. He looked down the path he had worn over the months. He saw Grandpa, frowning as he picked his way along it, unaware that his grandson was observing him.

How had he known where Paul was?

Was there a central office where information was

exchanged about children? All these months had passed, and Paul had imagined Daddy had forgotten his first explorations of the woods on Saturday mornings. That had been last summer and early fall. After that he had taken special measures to avoid being seen when he had come to spend an hour or so among the trees.

Had his father, glancing out of his office window, seen him in the late afternoons running or riding his bike across the bumpy ground of the meadow?

"There you are," his grandfather greeted him pleasantly. "I thought I might find you here."

Paul was mortified. They had sent someone after him. That the someone was his grandfather made it worse.

Grandpa sat down on a tree that had been a victim of the hard winter and lay toppled on the ground. He looked at Paul with an expression that was sympathetic yet grave.

"They sent you," Paul stated.

"Well—yes," Grandpa replied.

"To bring me back," Paul said.

Grandpa nodded.

"For the birthday . . ." Paul added lamely.

His grandfather glanced at the remains of the

stone wall, which showed up clearly because of the absence of foliage.

"Nice place you've got here," observed Grandpa.

He thought of Grandpa walking the mile and a half to the animal hospital, then cutting across the meadow.

"I think it's time for you to give it up," his grandfather said in a kindly way. "It's been going on for seven years. Of course you hardly planned it this way in the beginning. Jacob is an eerie child at times. He's irritating. You've explained him to yourself. It's the explanation you think you understand—not Jacob. That's true about other things as well. We're very familiar with our own explanations."

Paul shrugged.

"I think we'd best go," Grandpa said. "Unless you'd prefer to stay here in the woods?"

Was Grandpa giving him a real choice? He gauged the old man's expression. It was neutral.

Jacob's birthday was not important enough to Paul for him to make a big scene about it. Anyhow, Grandpa had acknowledged that Jacob was "eerie."

It was a small victory, but enough of one to persuade him to leave the woods, guiding his bike by its handlebars, following his grandfather down the path.

RADIANCE DESCENDING

Paul's father's Camry was parked at the curb in front of the animal hospital. He had thought Grandpa walked the mile and a half. But it was a day when his expectations, one by one, were not being fulfilled.

Grandpa drove with a certain restrained exuberance, catching traffic lights just as they were about to change, pushing on through the amber. Paul could tell his grandfather had been itching to get his hands on a steering wheel; you could see it in the way he looked intently through the windshield, a half-smile on his lips. They didn't talk during the five-minute drive.

When they arrived at the Coleman house, Paul was surprised to see how many cars were parked in the driveway, on the street, even at the edge of the lawn that sloped down in front of the house.

Had there been an accident?

Was Jacob sick? Had he been hurt?

Paul caught sight of a green balloon bobbing in a breeze that had sprung up and straining at the string that held it fastened to the knob on the front door.

Grandpa was silent as he parked the car in front of a neighbor's house and extricated himself from the driver's seat. He walked on ahead, not looking back to see whether Paul was following him.

Paul hesitated. He shoved his hands in his pockets and stood irresolutely on the sidewalk. His grandfather, seeming to sense his indecision, paused without turning to look at him. He was waiting in front of the walk that led to the Coleman front door. The green balloon, Paul noticed, had a stupid grinning face painted on it.

Better to get it over with, Paul said to himself, and with these words, found himself moving rapidly up the walk to the house, passing his grandfather on the way.

He pushed open the door, which was unlocked.

In the hall he found a crowd of people gathered

around the staircase. The noise of their conversations rose and fell like the tides of the sea.

They stood in groups of two and three. Paul recognized Dr. Newman, the counselor, and Josh, their former baby-sitter for Jacob, who had been to the barber during the last year and had his hair trimmed. There were the Pakistani owners of the newsdealer's store, the counterman and the plump cook from the delicatessen, the two young women from the Cards and Notions Shop, Dr. Brill himself, and Miss Greene from the public library.

Mrs. Brandy, Nora Coleman's elderly student, and her other student, the young man with the earrings, made a separate cluster, along with Molly, who kept watch over Jacob while Mrs. Coleman gave lessons on the piano.

It was Jacob's neighborhood.

Paul heard his mother's loud "Hush!" from the second floor. A second "Hush" followed—Jacob's voice, boisterous and hoarse and trembling with excitement.

Paul looked up along with everyone else as Jacob's steps on the stairs could be heard. He still came clumping down like a very small child, one foot joining the other on each stair step.

At the landing where the staircase turned, Jacob

appeared. He paused in front of the stained-glass window and looked down at the people, who grew silent at once.

Jacob blazed with the light that came through the window. He seemed made of gold and, like old drawings of the sun, his head was circled by spiky rays. He was dressed in a gold robe. He carried a golden staff in his right hand.

As though with one voice, people emitted a long, drawn-out "oooh."

Paul blinked.

His grandfather, who stood close behind him, whispered something to himself. "Radiance descending . . ." Paul thought he heard.

A minute later Jacob started down the last flight of stairs, which lay in shadow at that time of year.

Paul saw Jacob's costume plainly. Mom's handiwork was clumsy. One of the sun's rays, a small cone covered with gold paper, had worked itself loose and was hanging over Jacob's left eye, held to a band on his head by two coarse black threads. The gold robe had parted where the seam had unraveled. It revealed Jacob's blue jeans that had shrunk from dozens of washings. The gold paper had worked itself partly off the staff. Paul could see it was a rusty curtain rod.

Jacob reached the last step. People burst into the words of "Happy Birthday." He was hugged and kissed. Everyone who had to return to his or her business left; the others passed into the dining room, where a birthday lunch had been set out.

Jacob remained behind. He looked at Paul.

It was a look full of longing.

He took a step. Paul smelled lilac. Jacob's face bore the powdery marks of a big puff. He must have covered his cheeks with Mom's lilac dusting powder.

Paul's world had shifted ever so minutely. He was in a turmoil of new feelings, new thoughts. None of it made sense.

But an impulse took hold of him, and he stooped low enough for Jacob to tweak his nose with thumb and index finger. For such an awkward, shambling child, Jacob's touch on his nostrils was as light as two falling snowflakes.